To Me-Me, Barmy Jarmy,
Mr Chocolate, The Dragons,
Hard Rosemary and Harvey.

Blue Horse

HELEN STEPHENS

SCHOLASTIC PRESS • NEW YORK

Tilly was new in town,
and she didn't have
any friends yet.

So she stayed inside and
played all by herself.
It wasn't much fun playing
hide-and-seek . . .

when no one came to find her.

And when she played soccer . . .

no one kicked the ball back.

Then one day,
Tilly had a tea party.
There were no
guests to invite,
so she put Blue Horse
on a chair.
"One lump or two?"
she asked.

"Actually," said Blue Horse,
"I prefer my sugar lumps without any tea."
Tilly was very surprised. "You can talk!"

From then on,
Tilly and Blue Horse
were best friends.
They flew to the
moon, and Blue
Horse said Tilly was
the best astronaut he
had ever seen.

They went to
the Wild West,
where Tilly won
first prize in the
lassoing competition.

And when they went to the theater together,
Tilly wasn't scared . . .

even in the scariest scary parts.

One day, Tilly saw a girl alone in the park. "I wish I could say hello. But I'm too shy."

"Shy?" said Blue Horse. "You are the best astronaut I've ever seen. You won the Wild West lassoing competition. And you weren't even scared in the scariest scary parts!

"Go on. You can do it. I'll watch from here."

Tilly ran down to the park.
"Excuse me," she said.
"Would you like to play with me?"

"Okay," said the girl, whose name
was Pip. "But only if my friend
Wee Pip can play, too."

"Fantastic!" shouted Tilly. She called to Blue Horse, "Come down and meet my new friends!" So Blue Horse flew down.

And that afternoon Tilly made lots of new friends . . . and met *their* special friends, too!